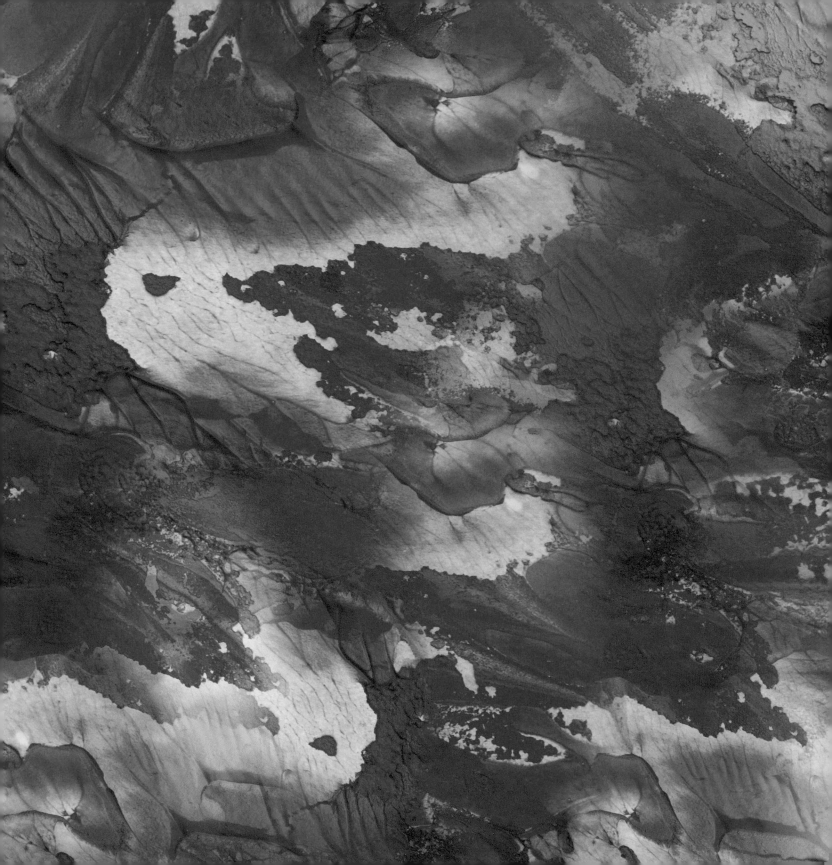

For my mom, Dollie Sorenson. —A.S.

For Uncle Bobby, who drew me pancakes every time I asked. —D.M.

Text Copyright © 2017 by Ashley N. Sorenson
Illustrations Copyright © 2017 by David Miles

Published by Familius LLC, www.familius.com

Familius books are available at special discounts for bulk purchases, whether for sales
promotions or for family or corporate use. For more information, contact Familius Sales at
559-876-2170 or email orders@familius.com. Reproduction of this book in any manner, in whole
or in part, without written permission of the publisher is prohibited.

Library of Congress Cataloging-in-Publication Data
2016958420   ISBN 9781944822828   eISBN 9781944822835

Illustrations done in mixed media on bristol board. Some elements used from Shutterstock.com.
Special thanks to Tucker Hawkins for his assistance.
Cover and book design by David Miles
Edited by Stephanie Yan

10 9 8 7 6 5 4 3 2 1   Printed in China   First Edition

COLOR BLOCKED

Ashley Sorenson

ILLUSTRATIONS BY

David Miles

Uh-oh.

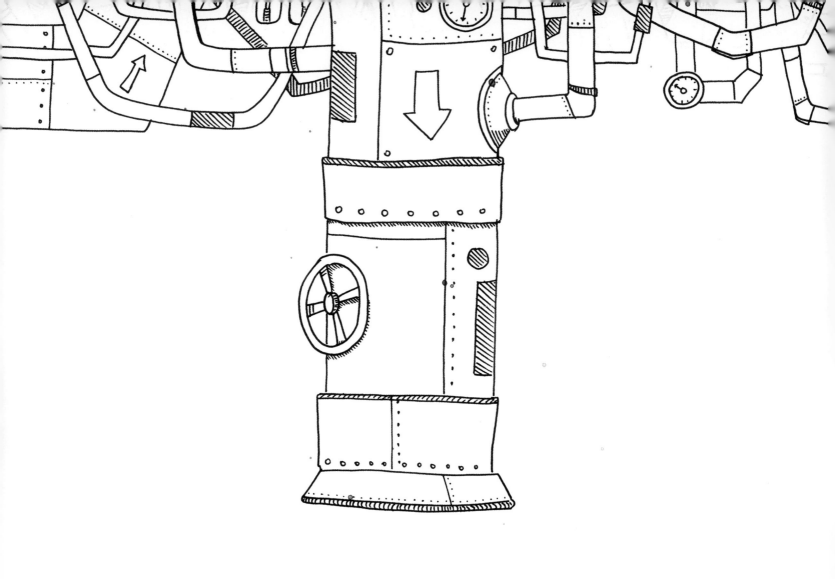

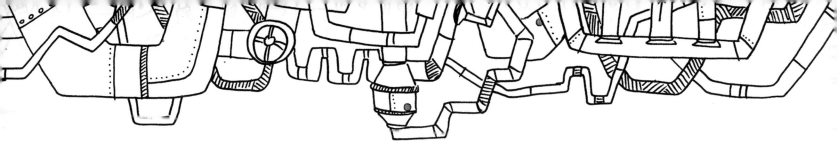

Color's blocked!

Gently shake this book from
side to side to unclog the pipe.

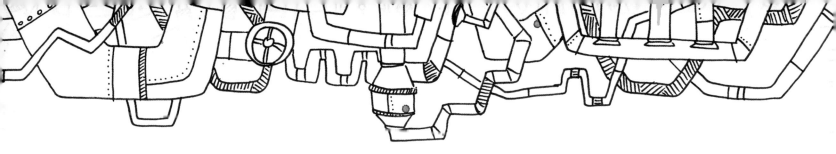

Hmm, that's odd.

Try shaking it up
and down this time.

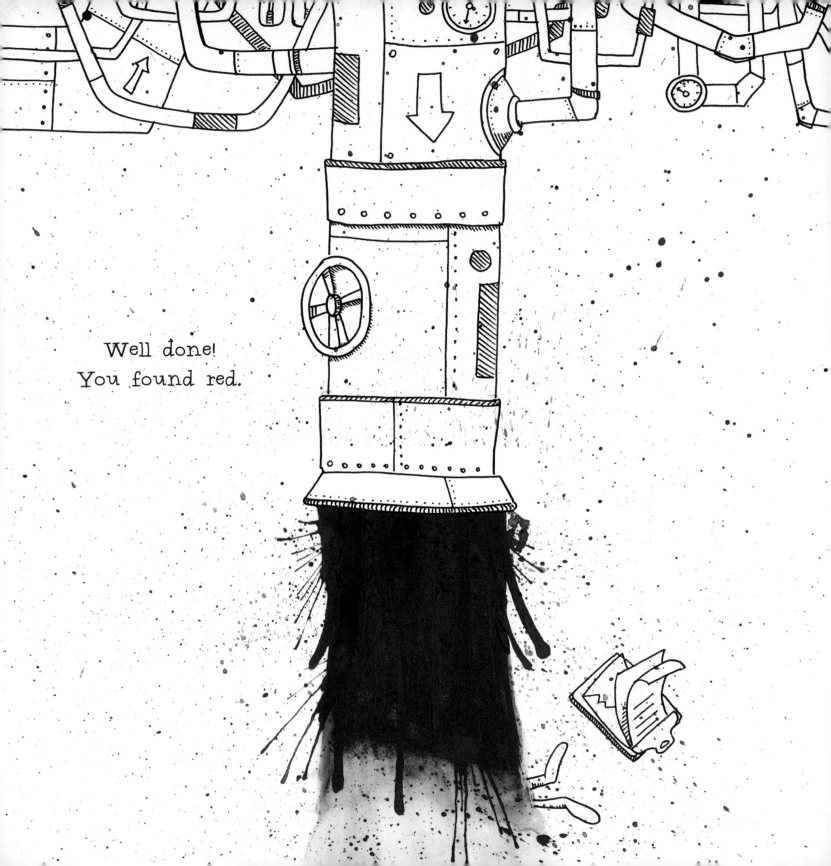

Well done!
You found red.

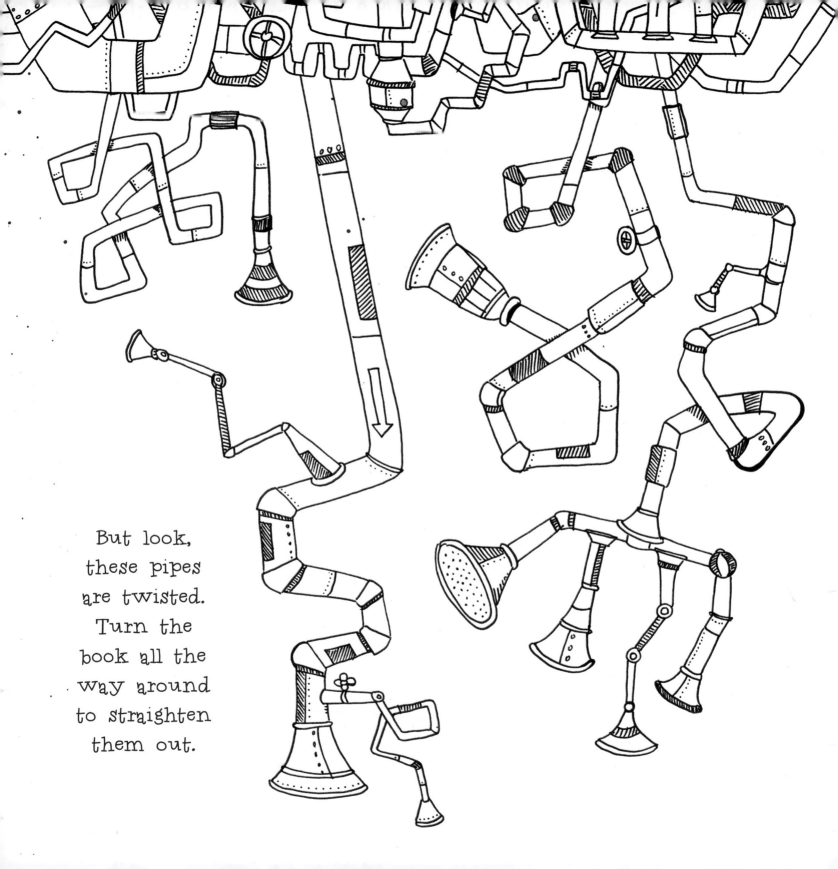

But look,
these pipes
are twisted.
Turn the
book all the
way around
to straighten
them out.

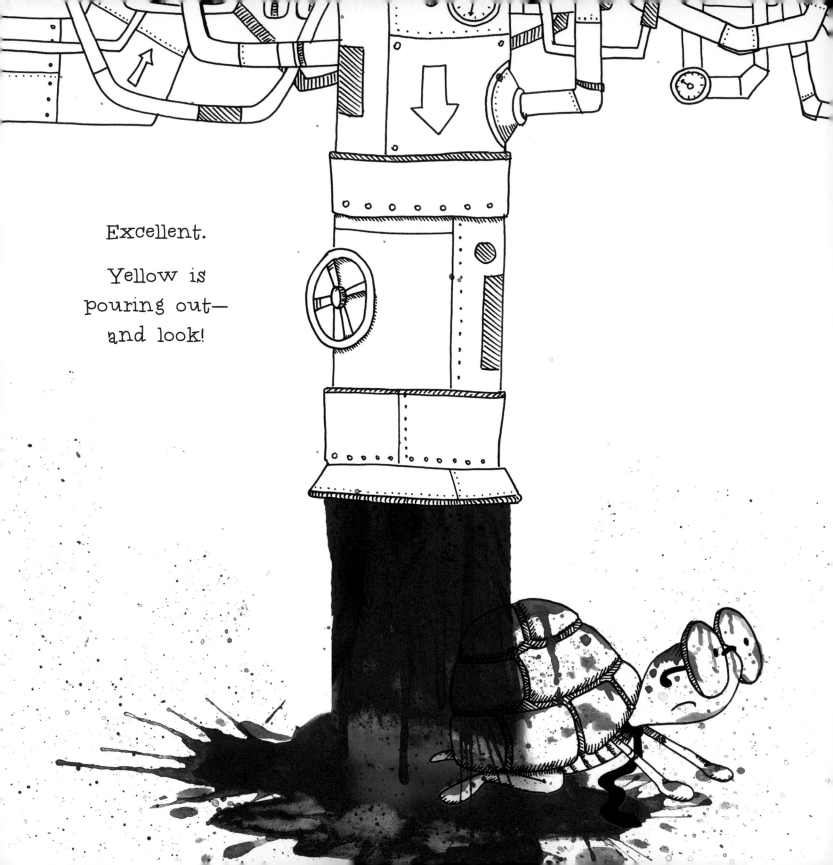

Excellent.

Yellow is
pouring out—
and look!

Yellow is mixing
with red and
turning orange.

Maybe that's too much. Turn the book sideways to dump some yellow out.

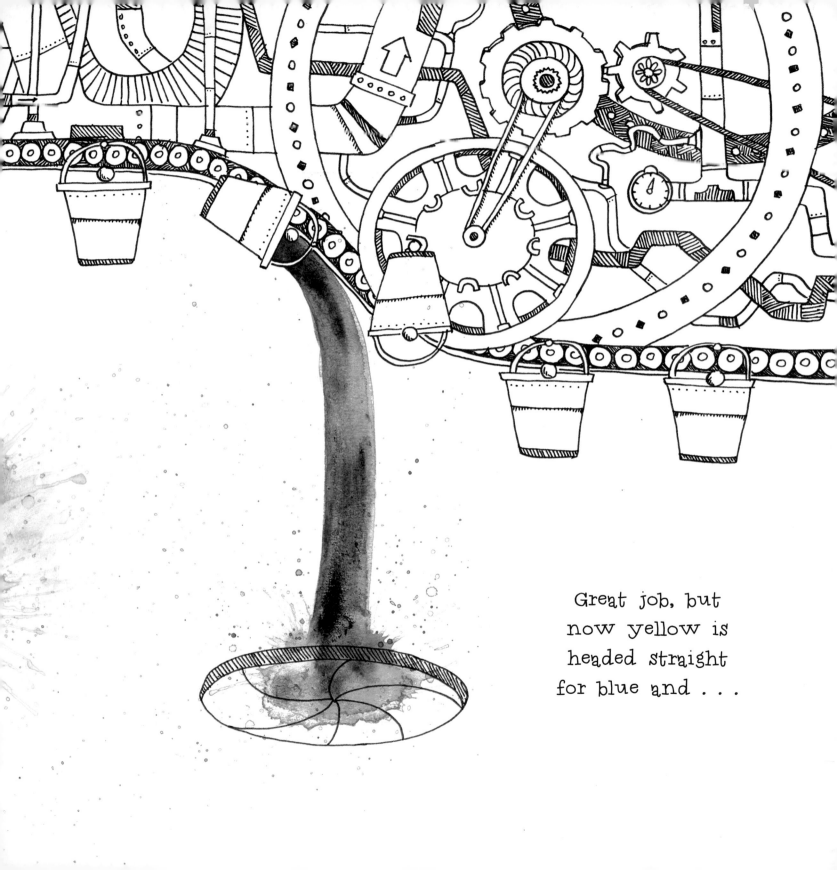

Great job, but now yellow is headed straight for blue and . . .

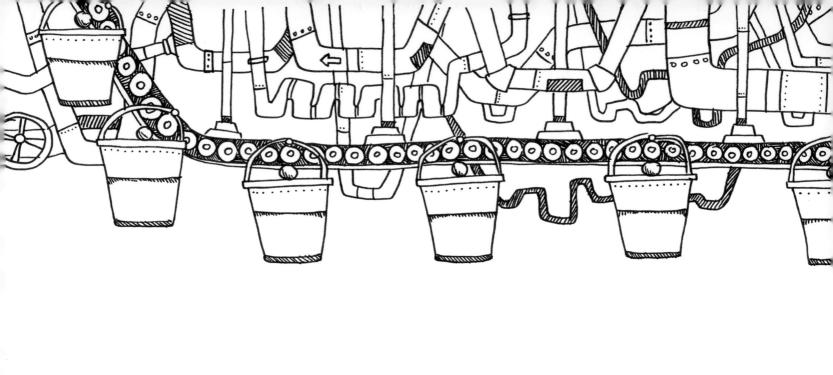

You guessed it.
Yellow and blue
are mixing to
make green.

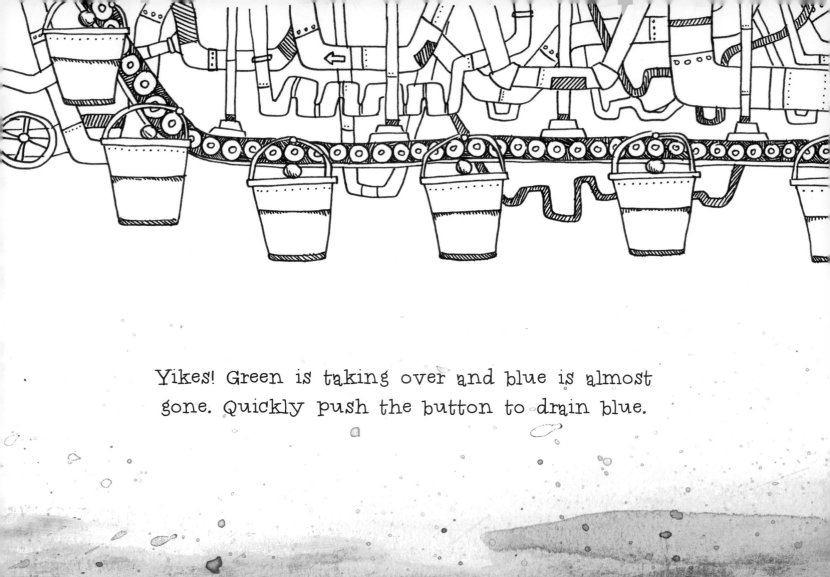

Yikes! Green is taking over and blue is almost gone. Quickly push the button to drain blue.

You saved blue! But now blue is dripping all over red. Rub the blue with your fingers to wipe it off.

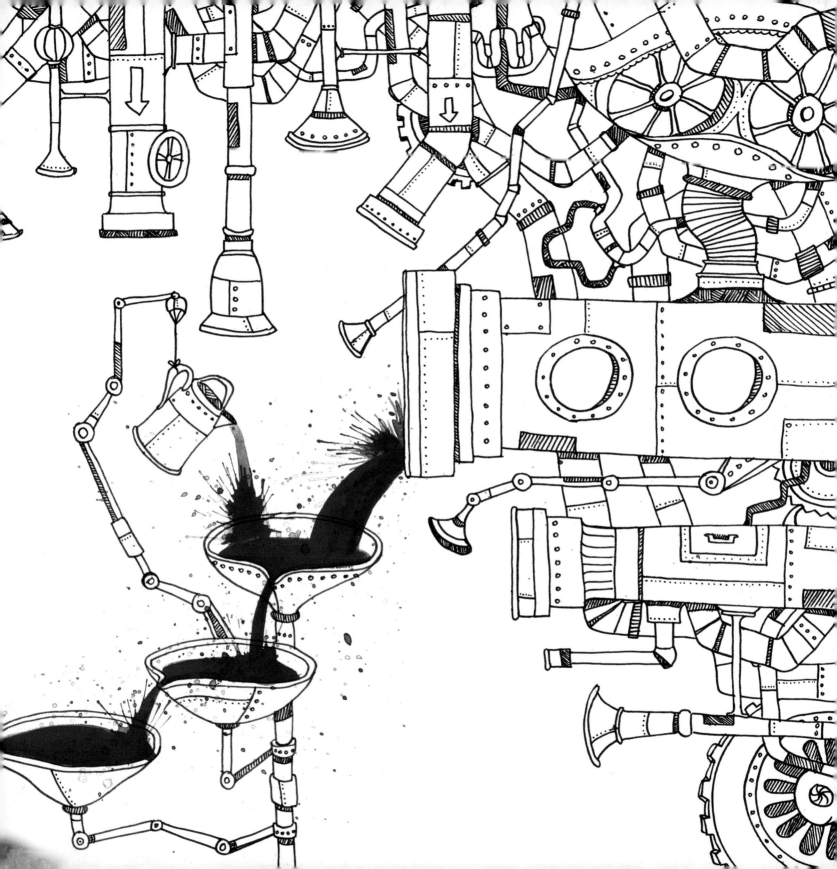

Oh dear. Blue
smeared with
red and turned
purple.

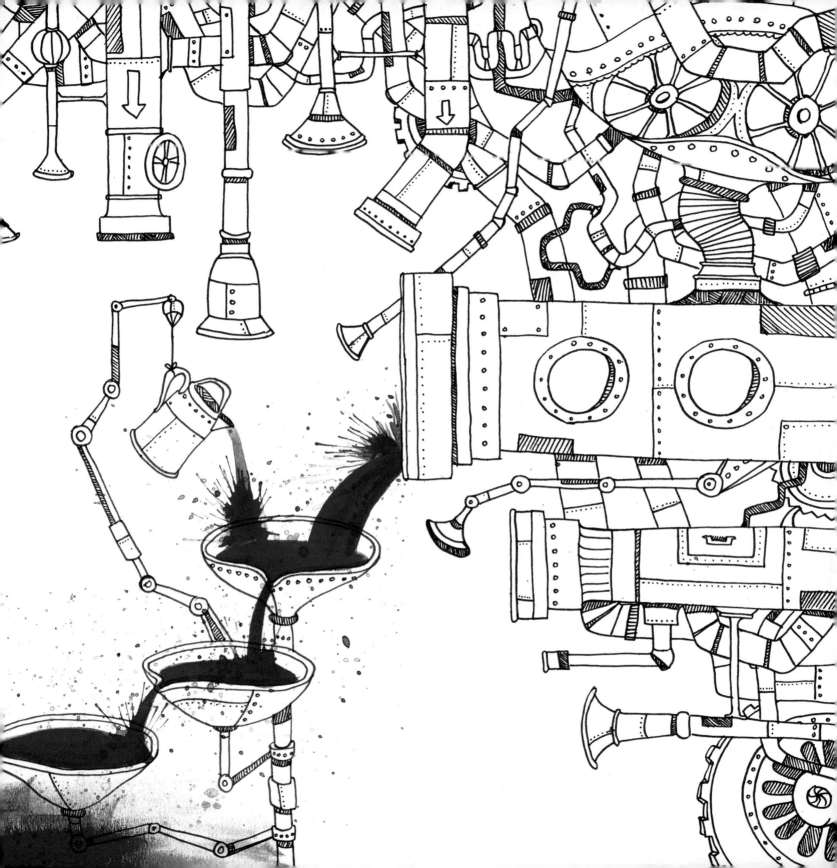

But wait, what's
that sound?

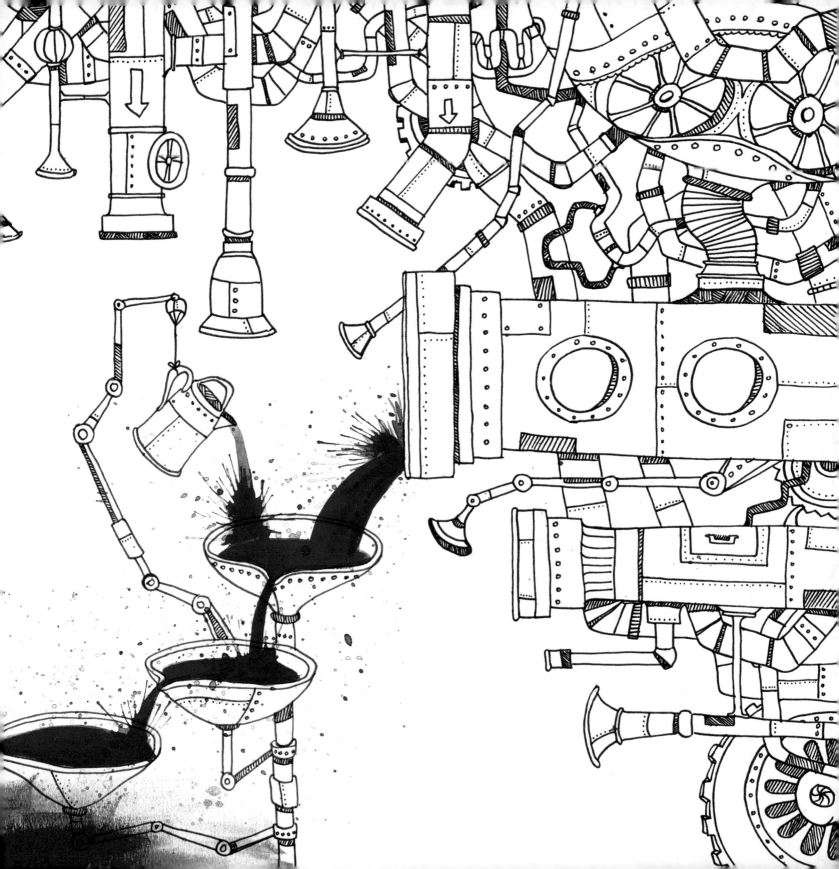

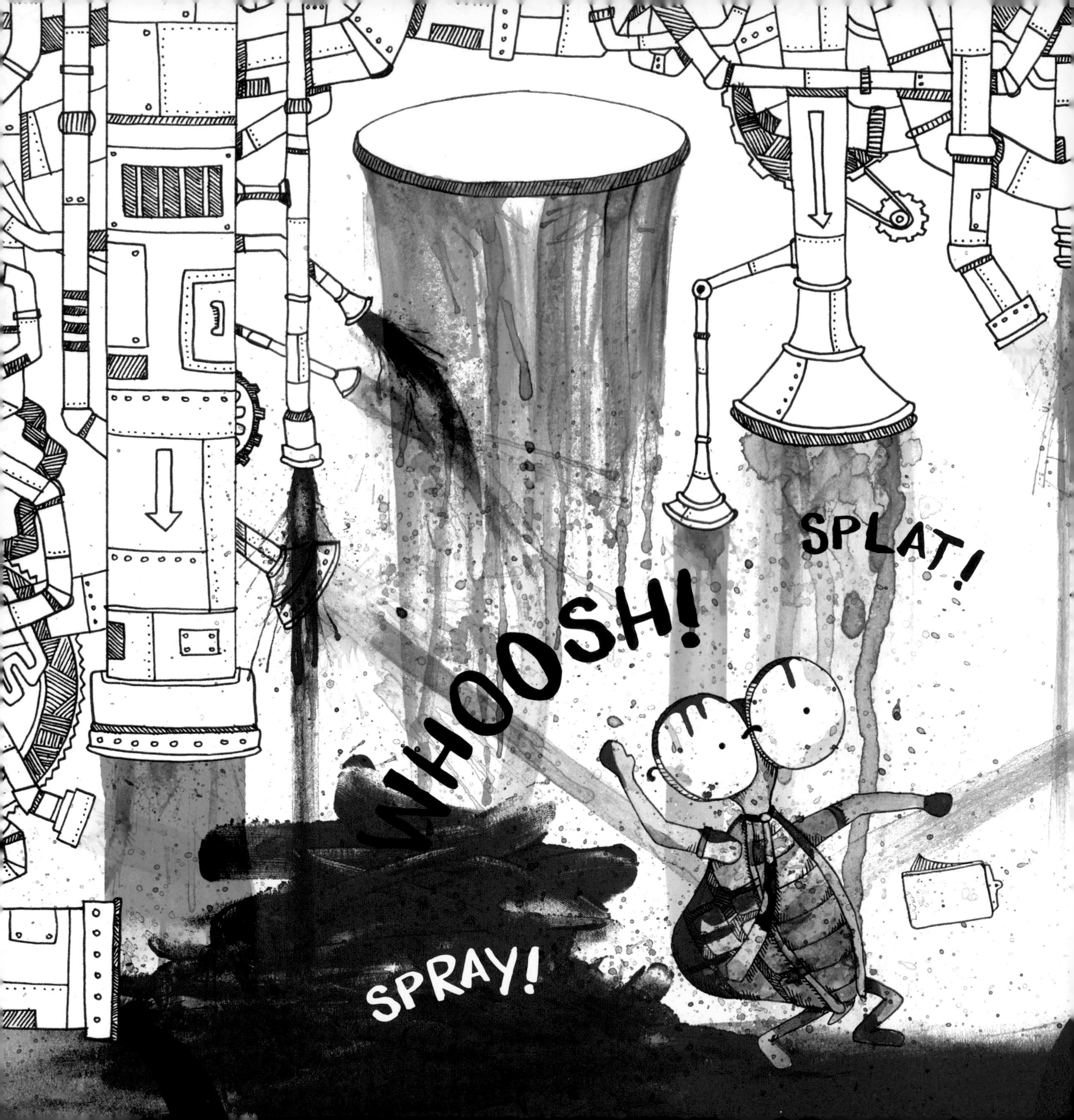
WHOOSH!
SPLAT!
SPRAY!

Quick, turn the book all the way around to close the pipes!

Oh no, the pipes
must be broken!

Color's exploding
everywhere!

Shut the book!

Shut the book!

Shut the boo